Meet the Characterz

Melvin Meadly

Daisy

DI Meadly

Priti Kaur

Worker 998

Zombee

Mr Johnson

Berty

Norman Crudwell

For Annette –
my kind and creative sister

OXFORD
UNIVERSITY PRESS

Great Clarendon Street, Oxford OX2 6DP

Oxford University Press is a department of the University of Oxford.
It furthers the University's objective of excellence in research, scholarship, and
education by publishing worldwide. Oxford is a registered trade mark of Oxford
University Press in the UK and in certain other countries

First published 2018

British Library Cataloguing in Publication Data

Data available

ISBN: 978-0-19-276389-1

1 3 5 7 9 10 8 6 4 2

Printed in China

Paper used in the production of this book is a natural,
recyclable product made from wood grown in sustainable forests.
The manufacturing process conforms to the environmental
regulations of the country of origin.

BEE BOY

Attack of the Zombees

Tony De Saulles

OXFORD

UNIVERSITY PRESS

If I tell anybody my secret I won't be allowed back. They made me promise — they told me:

Big troublezz if humanz findz out!

It's SO hard not to tell, but if I don't keep the secret...

I'LL NEVER BE A BEE AGAIN!

YOU'RE A BEE-KEEPER WHO CAN TURN INTO A BEE?

Yes! I know it sounds totally mad, but it's true. Sometimes, when my bees need me, I become one of them.

So here I am, puffing smoke into my hive. It calms the bees so I can check them without being stung, and sometimes – though it hasn't happened for ages – the smoke spirals around me, transforms me into a tiny bee, and takes me down into the hive. Will it happen today? I'm puffing and hoping and puffing and...

No. I don't think so.

But it's important that I check they're OK. I remove the roof and lift out a honeycomb frame. It's crawling with healthy-looking bees making honey. I check the lower frames where the queen lives. The cells are full of eggs and larvae.

I keep my hive on the roof of Meadow Tower, a block of flats where I live with Mum.
Just like Meadow Tower, my hive is full of busy workers - some cleaning, others nursing, other gathering food, guarding, or sometimes even fighting, and - HANG ON, SOMEONE'S COMING...

WHAT ARE YOU DOING UP HERE?

It's Mum.

NO BEES BEFORE SCHOOL. I WON'T TELL YOU AGAIN, MELVIN!

She's not usually this stressed. I think it's her work. Mum has to deal with a lot of difficult stuff – robberies, car crashes, missing people, and looking after me. Being a detective inspector for the police *and* a mum is a difficult mix.

'Nearly finished, Mum...'

WELL, HURRY UP, LOVE. I'M OFF TO THE STATION. BEE SUIT OFF, EAT SOME BREAKFAST, AND DON'T FORGET TO LOCK UP!

Miss Springfield

School has definitely improved in the last few weeks. We have a new teacher, Miss Springfield. She's into nature and animals and bugs... and bees, of course. Most of my mates think bees are cool too. But that's quite a new thing. A few weeks ago, everybody in class thought bees and bee-keepers were rubbish! Let's just say we get on better now. I even have a best friend – Priti Kaur. She's brainy, brave, and funny too.

Priti lives a few floors below us in Meadow Tower. We walk to school together most days.

'Hey, Mel, look!'

We've reached the school gates, and Priti's pointing at a big car pulling up outside reception, where a crowd is waiting.

'It's a Rolls-Royce!' she says, admiring the posh motor.

The driver is wearing a peaked cap. He walks round to the side of the Rolls and opens the door.

A boy steps out. He looks like he's from a boy band, with his trendy hair, golden trainers, and a hoodie with golden cuffs!

The boy is smiling faintly. He glances around, soaking in his surroundings, as journalists push and jostle for position, snapping photos and scribbling in notepads. TV cameras are capturing the event.

How long will you be at St John's?

Do you mind being away from home?

Why are staying with your uncle?

When does he next appear on telly?

Are those trainers real gold?

Is it true you're going to be a pop superstar?

But the boy ignores them.

Priti is staring open-mouthed. 'Wow!' she says, and, for a moment, I hate him. This is totally ridiculous because I don't even know the boy!

'There's Suzy Skittles off the TV news!' I say to divert attention.

Suzy has pushed her way to the front. 'What's it like having such a famous and successful uncle?' she asks, smiling kindly.

The boy looks up for the first time. 'We are a successful family,' he says. 'I guess I'll be a celebrity like my uncle when I'm older.'

Then our head teacher butts in. Mrs Bottomly claps her hands and talks to the reporters like they're year ones!

'Let the new boy through, please! I have a press information sheet, BUT YOU WON'T GET IT IF YOU DON'T STAND BACK!'

Like scolded children, the reporters quieten down and move aside to allow the boy through.

An hour later they are back in their offices, writing their stories.

DAiLY NEWS

HEIR TO CRUMP FORTUNE STARTS NEW SCHOOL TODAY!

Berty Crump, nephew of TV celebrity and millionaire businessman Sir Crispin Crump, was delivered to St John's Primary School in a Rolls-Royce this  morning. Controversial Sir Crispin, who shot to fame with his hit TV show *Get Rich Quick!*, was unable to accompany his nephew. In a statement, he explained:

'*I'm sorry that I couldn't take Berty to his new school, but I have other commitments filling my busy schedule. I'm setting up an exciting new project on the edge of town, but will, of course, do my very best to look after young Berty while he stays in Crump Mansion for a few months.*'

'Melvin!' It's Miss Springfield, and she's holding Berty Crump's hand. 'This is Berty. I'd like you to look after him today – be his special friend. You can introduce him to the other children, show him outside at break, and take him to lunch. Will you do that for me?'

I'd do pretty much anything for Miss Springfield.

'Yes, Miss,' I say.

'And I'll help!' Priti adds, as Miss Springfield heads back inside.

'Hi, Berty!' I offer to shake his hand.

'Special friend?' he laughs, and smiles at Priti. 'I have plenty of friends, thanks, and who shakes hands? We're not fifty!'

I stick my hands in my pockets. My classmates swarm around the new boy, and we head for our first lesson.

I'm pretty sure Berty Crump doesn't like me, but Miss Springfield has asked me to look after him, and I won't let her down.

When his name is called at register, Berty says, 'Yo!' Miss Springfield looks up with surprise. We're supposed to say, 'Yes, Miss!', but she lets it go.

At break, Berty sits in the playground checking his phone for messages and refusing to kick a ball around with us.

'We're not allowed mobiles at school,' I say, to save him from getting into trouble.

'Uncle got permission from Old Bottoms!' he replies. 'Special people, special rules, and all that.'

Old Bottoms?

Then I realize he's talking about our headmistress!

'What are your hobbies?' I ask, to change the conversation.

'You mean, what am I into? Playing guitar and writing music, mostly,' Berty says.

A cluster of our classmates have gathered round to earwig our conversation. Even troublemaker Norman Crudwell looks star-struck as Berty's boasting continues. 'I'll be appearing on *Tons of Talent* this year. Uncle Crispin knows the producer,' he says, and the crowd gasps with admiration at the soon-to-be superstar.

Priti has a wide-eyed, startled expression, like she can't believe how amazing Berty Crump is. I can't let him win her over.

Time to tell him about my bees, I reckon. He's not the only one with hidden talents.

'My nickname is Bee Boy!' I announce. 'And I keep bees on the roof of Meadow Tower!'

But it doesn't have the effect I'm hoping for.

Berty jumps up. 'BEES?' he shouts. 'YOU KEEP BEES?'

'Er, yeah...' I start to explain, but Berty Crump's in my face.

'I HATE BEES!' he hisses. 'I hate all bugs actually, but BEES? Ugh – GROSS!'

And he stomps off, with a trail of tutting fans close behind.

Priti elbows me gently in the side. 'Rich twit!' she says, and I feel bad for imagining that Berty could have impressed her.

17

The new boy has cheered up a bit by the time I take him to the school hall for lunch.

We're queuing with our trays. Berty is behind Priti and me. We both choose pizza, and for pudding there's a choice of honey sponge or yogurt. I sniff the honey sponge.

Smells odd.

I'm super fussy about my honey, and this pudding doesn't smell right. The smell isn't bad, it's just wrong. I can't explain why, but I advise Priti and Berty not to eat it. Priti chooses a yogurt, but Berty's not happy.

'I don't need you to tell me what I can and can't eat, thank you, Bee Man!' he snaps, and slops a bowl of honey sponge pudding on his tray.

18

'Yeah, BEE MAN!' Crudwell chips in, from further down the queue. 'Mind your own BEESNESS!'

'Too right!' Berty chuckles at the lame joke, and Crudwell smirks with pride, grabbing a bowl of the suspicious sponge for himself.

Priti and I raise our eyebrows but say nothing.

We sit in silence. Well, not total silence – there's a lot of chomping and slurping from Berty and Norman Crudwell as they munch their lunch. Am I imagining it, or have their faces turned a bit yellow?

19

After lunch, the tables are cleared and there's an assembly to welcome Berty to St John's. We're busily chatting but look up when Mrs Bottomly walks to the middle of the stage. She raises her hand, and the chattering fades to silence.

'Today is a special day,' she announces. 'I am very pleased to welcome a new pupil to St John's.' Mrs Bottomly is glowing with pride. 'Would you like to come up, please, young man?'

Berty Crump hops on to the stage, grinning and waving like royalty.

But the grin quickly
fades as Berty
clutches his stomach.

Mrs Bottomly's
glow has also
faded. 'Er, please
introduce yourself
to . . . er, the school,'
she says.

I didn't imagine it – poor Berty is
definitely looking yellow. His confidence
seems to have leaked away, and now he
just looks . . . ill.

'Hi,' he mutters. His cheeks inflate. 'My
name is Ber . . . B – B – Ber . . .'

Berty Crump is sick on the stage (and Mrs Bottomly's shoes).

'Oh Berty – B – B – B …' Mrs Bottomly's face has turned yellow too. She stares down at the sea of little faces, with a boggle-eyed expression…

BLURRRGH!

Chaos breaks out.

The hall is filled with shrieking children. Half of them (including Norman Crudwell) have yellow faces too, and, like Berty Crump and Mrs Bottomly, they are sick.

Meanwhile, in a secret laboratory on the edge of town...

'You reckon it was the honey sponge pudding?' Priti asks, on the way home.

'Maybe,' I say. 'It did smell a bit odd.'

'Trust you to notice, Bee Boy!' Priti laughs. 'I didn't smell anything.'

'We didn't eat it, and we weren't sick,' I say.

Priti shrugs. 'True. I hope Berty's OK.'

'Not just him,' I say. 'All the kids!'

Priti agrees. 'Well, the sickness didn't last long, and their yellow skin quickly changed back to normal.'

It's true. But school still had to finish early, with teachers busy phoning parents — and, of course, there was LOTS of mopping up to do.

Priti goes up to her flat when we reach Meadow Tower, but I don't go home. There's somebody I need to visit.

Dan

Last year, Dan moved next door and became our friend. It was Dan who got me into bee-keeping. He found an old hive at the dump, and after he'd fixed it up we filled it with bees. It was going really well, but then Dan left and I had to keep going on my own. I had a bit of a battle with my neighbours at first. They didn't want me keeping bees on the roof of Meadow Tower and... well... stuff happened. Horrible stuff, actually. But it's sorted now, and I'm managing OK without Dan.

But it's not Dan I'm visiting; it's Daisy, his mum.

27

It was Daisy who gave us the bees. She keeps six hives at the bottom of her garden, so if she's not in her house I know where I'll find her.

'Have you ever heard of people getting sick from eating honey, Daisy?' I ask.

'Never!' Daisy says. 'But bees sometimes get sick when they feed on plants that have been treated with chemicals. Farmers want to get rid of the bugs and weeds that spoil their crops, but useful insects sometimes get harmed too.'

'Like bees?'

'Yes! Plants need pollinating insects, and so do farmers. No bees, no crops!'

'And the sickness?' I ask.

'Who knows?' Daisy says. 'But if bees are taking nectar and pollen from sprayed plants, maybe sick bees make sick honey?'

'Dan would know!' I say.

That's why Dan left. He works in other countries, helping scientists who are trying to figure out why so many bees are dying. It's happening all around the world, so it's an important job.

'I'm not sure Dan has the answers yet,' Daisy says.

'Did you see the photo?' I ask.

Dan keeps in touch by sending emails.

'The bee beard? Yes, hilarious! But I don't want you trying that!' Daisy laughs.

Daisy likes chatting about her son – he's a sort of link between us. But Daisy's busy with her bees, so I don't stay long.

'Don't forget, Mel,' she calls out, as I'm walking back up the path, 'look after your bees, and they'll look after you!'

〈⬡⬡⬡⬡⬡⬡〉

I'm back on the roof of Meadow Tower.

Mum and Mr Johnson are chatting by my beehive. 'Did you see that giant bee

on the TV news?' Mr Johnson says.
'Somebody in town got stung on the arm!'

'A giant bee? Are they OK?' Mum asks.

'Said in the newspaper that they turned
yellow for a few minutes!' Mr Johnson
laughs. 'But you know what newspapers
are like.'

'Might have been a hornet,' Mum says.
'They're pretty big.'

'Or even one of those Asian hornets?'
I chip in.

Mr Johnson grows tomatoes and other vegetables in pots on the roof and keeps an eye on my beehive when I'm at school. But he's finished watering his plants, so Mum invites him downstairs for a cup of tea, which is excellent because I like checking the bees on my own.

Five minutes later, I'm puffing my smoker and hoping, hoping, hoping that the smoke will work its magic again.

Mr Johnson was helping me check my hive when it first happened. So how did I keep it a secret if he was watching? Well, that's the weird thing. Time seemed to stand still, and Mr Johnson didn't even notice I'd disappeared...

WAIT!

The smoke is curling.
It's wrapping
around me...

IT'S HAPPENING!

Yes...that floaty feeling. I'm weightless,
drifting down, down, down...

FLOOMF!

Here I am again. Welcome, Marzter!

I am with my bees. It's dark and warm, and there's that lovely sweet, smoky smell. A happy buzz sizzles through my body, and, looking down at my legs and... wings... I see that once more:

I AM BEE BOY!

A bee steps forward, smaller than the others but with the confident look of a leader. She reminds me of 33137, a brave friend from my first swarm.

'I'z bee number 998, Marzter. Youz save our swarm, gave uzz new home!' she says, and the others join in.

Save swarm!

Zank you, Marzter!

'46664 do waggle dance,' 998 continues. 'Follow uzz!'

We cross the honeycomb floor to join another group of bees, watching 46664 as she wiggles around, following an invisible number eight on the floor.

35

The dance is not for fun: it shows us in what direction and how far away a source of food is. The food is nectar and pollen that is stored in flowers.

46664 is very excited. The flowers she has discovered fill a whole field, and they are big... VERY BIG!

'Will youz come wiz uzz, Marzter?' 998 asks.

There's no way I'm going to miss this! We follow the light to the entrance. Then we're out into the brightness and away, spiralling up above Meadow Tower.

I look down at our flat and the school.
Look — there's Miss Springfield, walking
across the playground to her little electric car!

We fly to the edge of town and follow
the line of Frogmarsh Lane. At the far
end looms a dark factory, sitting in front
of a wood. The building has sooty walls
with black windows and doors.

In the middle of the woods behind the factory is a secret field filled with colour.
Flowerz, Marzter!
Just like I told youz!

Zooming closer, we see that the flowers are gigantic!

There is a clearing in the middle of the field, with a black windowless building in the centre.

Rising out of the roof is a control tower with a large sphere three-quarters of the way up. Bee-like drones are taking off from the sphere and spraying the field with a shower of yellow liquid before disappearing back inside to refill. On top of the tower shines a huge sun ball.

Figures in shiny metal bee-keeper suits are busy on the ground. Some seem to be mechanics servicing the drones, while others emerge from the black building with flowers for planting outside.

We fly down to take a closer look.

'Building iz greenhouz!' 998 says.

And she's right. It is made from glass — black on the outside but clear on the inside, so you can see out but you can't see in. We buzz closer.

Through the open doors we see giant sun lamps hanging from the ceiling and pipes with shower heads for watering. A shiny-suited bee-keeper hits a big red button on the wall, and the plant pots are

This is no ordinary greenhouse — it's some sort of super-hothouse. I'M GETTING A BAD FEELING ABOUT THIS PLACE.

But 46664 and the rest of the bees are very excited as we leave the hothouse and explore the delicious flowers.

'Stop!' I shout. 'Leave the flowers alone!'

The bees are surprised.

'NO!' 998 is firm.
'Marzter zay stop,
so weez stop!'

The bees are surprised, but they obey
little 998. All except one.

46664 just can't resist. She discovered the
field of tasty flowers, and she's not going
to stop now.

'46664! Please, don't!' I say.
But she can't hear me. Her
head is buried deep in a giant
yellow poppy, and she is greedily
slurping up nectar. Then she
leaves the poppy and hovers
over a new flower.

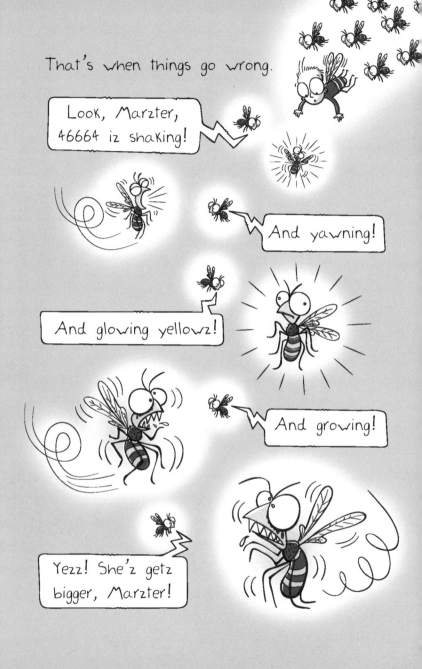

It's true. 46664 is expanding before our eyes. She's glowing yellow, and her yawns have turned into growls!

GRARRZZZZZ!

And as she screams her battle cry, other glowing monster bees emerge from the flowers. Their faces are set in a dead expression as they circle around us preparing to attack!

Our only escape is to whizz up, up, up until the sun ball is just a glowing dot below.

49

But the monster swarm is lightning fast.

They've curved up and around us. They're attacking from above, chasing us back down to the hothouse and are closing in fast.

We need a plan. It's do or DIE!

The sun ball is growing rapidly as we zoom downwards.

Think, think...

What if we...

Yes, that's it!

FOLLOW ME!

I'm shouting instructions as we hurtle down to the sun ball.

Will the monster bees fall for our trap? They don't look too clever, with their weird expressions!

We smother the glowing ball and arrange ourselves to look like...

51

Another bee! But this one is even larger than the big bees chasing us.

Here they come.

'Don't move until I say!' I shout.

'GO!' I scream, half a second before they hit us. And as we whizz to safety, our giant attackers smash into the glowing sun ball and sizzle to a crisp.

It worked! We've won – for now. But I'm certain there are more bees ready to attack, so it's time to leave. We fly fast over traffic and trees, heading home to our hive.

My insect friends are pleased to be alive, but I feel bad. We had to kill other bees to survive.

'Poor 46664!' I say.

'It'z sad, Marzter,' 998 replies. 'But youz saved uzz. Weez ALL could have died!'

We're back, and I'm standing by my hive on the roof of Meadow Tower. Not a bee, but a boy again.

∞∞∞∞∞∞∞

Everybody is back at school. The sickness bug was soon gone. Mrs Bottomly asked everybody not to discuss the unfortunate illness outside school, as she was keen to shield Berty Crump from harmful publicity.

'The school must protect all pupils,' Mrs Bottomly said. 'Famous or not!'

She explained that the kitchens were checked and given the all-clear, and, thankfully, so far, the newspapers hadn't found out.

'Thank goodness I've got such a lovely, NORMAL son!' Mum said when I told her. 'There's nothing worse than people thinking they're special!'

55

But I'm not bothered about celebrity rich kids. I'm worried about the field in Frogmarsh Lane. What's that all about? Giant flowers, drones spraying chemicals, bee-keepers in metal suits, the dark factory, and the black hothouse with the shining sun ball? And what about those giant glowing bees with their dead, zombie-like expressions?

Maybe that's it. They're not zombies... they're zomBEES!

'How about you, Melvin?' Miss Springfield asks. 'What have you brought in for us?'

'He's daydreaming, Miss,' Norman Crudwell shouts from the back of the class.

'Yes, thank you, Norman,' Miss Springfield says. 'Perhaps you'd like to tell us about YOUR contribution?'

It's our weekly 'Show and Tell' session, where we bring something of interest from home and discuss it with the class.

Crudwell doesn't normally bring anything, but today he is wobbling to the front of the class with a pot plant.

'It's my Venus flytrap, Miss!' he says.
'It eats flies and...'

Crudwell looks across at me.

'How interesting! A carnivorous plant!'
Miss Springfield gasps.

'Don't know if it's *car-nivvy-ous*, Miss.'
Crudwell looks confused. 'But it eats meat!'

Berty Crump is excited. 'A bee-eating
plant? Excellent! Where did you get it?'

Norman Crudwell puffs with pride at the

posh boy's approval and
waggles a little paper envelope.

seeds

'Mum grows them from seeds on our
kitchen windowsill,' he explains. 'They
scoff any bees that invade our house.'

Invade? That's a bit dramatic! Bees want
to be in gardens, not houses and flats.

Miss Springfield is so pleased with
Crudwell's contribution that she decides
to feature the plant in our science lesson.
We sketch flytraps, drawing the detail
of their spikes and little trigger hairs.
Then we watch a video showing flytraps
snapping shut on juicy bugs and dissolving
their bodies in digestive juice. Later, using
tweezers, Berty brushes a tiny bit of meat
across the trigger hairs, and the trap snaps
shut. The whole class shrieks with delight
– except me. Crudwell's Venus flytrap plant
is amazing, but there's no way I'm going

to let him see that I'm impressed.
Berty Crump slaps Crudwell on the back.
'Totally brilliant!' he laughs. 'Watching
your flytraps eating their lunch has made
me hungry too!'

Norman Crudwell sniggers and nods with
agreement.

Which is good timing because that's when
the lunch bell rings.

I'm studying the puddings
while Mrs Sweed, the
school cook, slops a portion
of pasta bake on to my
plate. The choice of puds
today is fruit or honey
roly-poly and custard.

I shut my eyes
and sniff.

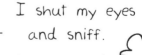

THE SAME SMELL!

Priti spots the pudding and looks at me.

I shake my head.

But silent communication doesn't work with Berty Crump.

'How about an apple, Berty?' I say, trying not to sound bossy.

But Berty loves his puddings. 'Oh great, it's the dinner police again!' he sneers. 'So what's wrong with the roly-poly pud, Detective Bee Man?'

Crudwell's head appears over Berty's shoulder. 'Yeah, Bee Man, what's wrong with it?' he hisses.

I shrug. 'Just wondered if it was the honey sponge pudding that made you ill last time,' I say.

'They checked the kitchens, didn't they?' Berty argues, snatching a bowl of the steaming pud and waving it under my nose. 'Anyway, I doubt Old Bottoms would risk letting me get ill again!'

'No, but...' I try to explain.

'Roly-poly is the best pudding in the world!' Crudwell punches the air.

'Calm down,' Berty says, sneering at his overenthusiastic fan.

I have a feeling this isn't going to go well. Should I warn a teacher about the pudding? Miss Springfield, perhaps? But if all I can say is 'It smells funny, Miss!', they're not going to throw it in the bin.

Priti waves for me to join her at the long table. Berty sits at the far end with Crudwell and some of his other admirers.

And, of course, it happens again – but much quicker this time.

Berty hasn't even finished his roly-poly pudding when his face starts to glow yellow. And then he's ill, but this time it's not sick gushing from his mouth, it's dribble.

He tries mopping it on his sleeve first, and then with a tissue, but the dribble keeps flowing. Poor yellow-faced Berty drools into his overflowing pudding bowl. I see Norman Crudwell and all the other roly-poly eaters are having the same problem. The dribble is unstoppable. They're clutching their mouths trying to stop the flow, but the yellow goo is spreading over tables, dripping off the edges, and splattering into yellow puddles on the floor.

It's revolting, but fascinating! Priti grabs my arm. 'Let's get out of here!' she says.

We escape with the other non-dribblers and watch through windows from the dry corridor. Teachers and dinner ladies gather the yellow-faced children, and, slipping and sliding, they escape outside to the safety of the playground.

The dribbling finishes as quickly as it started, and bright yellow faces soon fade back to normal. Dinner ladies mop up the gunge, and teachers calm the children, checking that everybody is OK.

'It MUST be the pudding,' I tell Priti.

'Let's investigate!' she says, and we head for the school kitchen.

Standing on chairs, Priti and I peer through a round window in the kitchen door.

'It's Mrs Sweed,' Priti whispers. 'She's having an argument!'

'That's Tom, her son,' I say. 'Look at the jar she's holding!'

Mrs Sweed is waving a jar at her son. It's an unusual hexagonal shape — like a big honeycomb cell with a lid.

'No more, Tom!' she shouts. 'You said this batch was OK, but it's made the children ill — AGAIN!'

Tom Sweed looks worried. 'B-b-but we have to test it, Mum. If I don't help him, I'll lose my job... or worse!'

'What about MY job?' Mrs Sweed replies. 'There'll be trouble this time. I won't get away with it twice!'

'Can you read the label?' I ask Priti.

'No!' she whispers. 'But it MUST be honey.'

It's Miss Springfield.

'I don't know what you're up to, and to be honest,' she sighs, 'I don't have time to find out. Everybody's feeling better now, but school is finishing early. We've tried phoning Sir Crispin, but he's busy in a meeting. Would you two mind walking Berty home?'

Priti and I exchange glances.

'Yes, Miss,' we reply.

Berty is looking pale and a little bit
embarrassed when we meet him by reception.
I want to say 'I warned you!', but I
keep quiet. The three of us set off across
the playground, with Priti and Berty in front.

I spot something on
the ground. It's an
envelope — Norman
Crudwell's Venus
flytrap seeds! I slip
them in my pocket and
run to catch up.

'Suzy Skittles!' Priti gasps, as we
approach the school gates.

'She must have heard about the dribble
sickness!' I say. 'Don't let her see Berty!'

And, for once, Berty follows my advice. We
turn his hoodie inside out, pull the hood over
his head, and put his trainers in his rucksack.

Berty stares at the ground as we try to sneak past the TV reporter.

'Hey, you three!' Suzy Skittles runs over. 'What's going on in there? What's this I hear about a dribbling sickness?'

I cough, hoping she might think it's catching. 'Yeah, it's not that bad, but we need to get home.'

Suzy steps back. 'Oh, right. Do you know if Berty Crump was sick? Do you think his uncle will make a complaint?'

I remember Mrs Bottomly's warning about talking to the newspapers, and I'm praying Berty won't say anything. Thankfully, he stays undercover.

I guess if you dream of being a pop star, you don't want the world to know that you've been dribbling like a baby. He coughs loudly, and Priti joins in.

'Sorry,' I splutter, 'but we need to go.'

Priti and I hook arms with Berty to speed up our escape, but Suzy Skittles doesn't give up easily.

She pushes a business card in the pocket of Priti's satchel as we scurry off.

'If you hear anything, let me know!' she shouts.

We keep our heads down and hurry along, but we are being followed. We hear a buzzing sound and look round to see a giant bee heading straight for us.

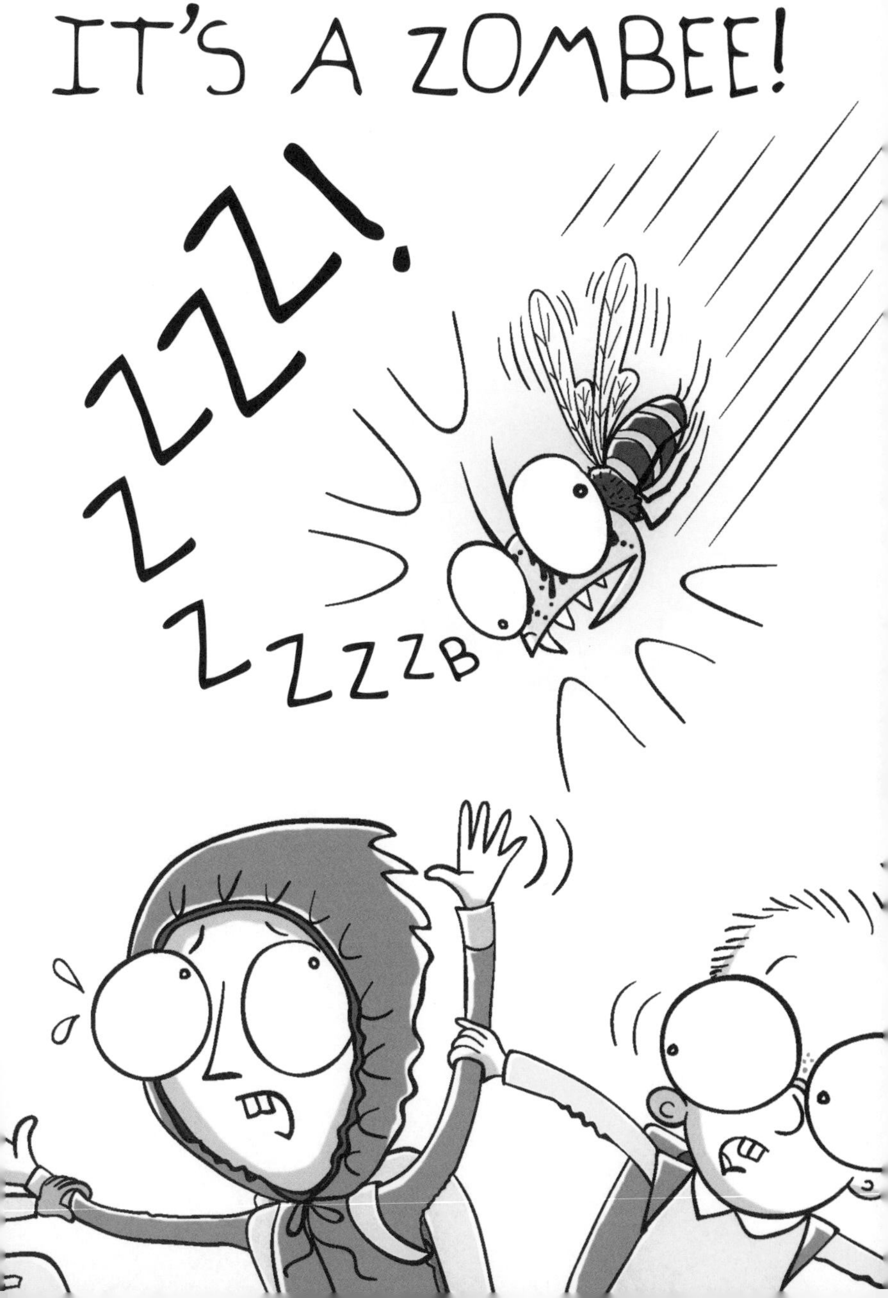
IT'S A ZOMBEE!
ZZZZ!
ZZZZZZZB

We duck, and it whizzes past but turns and comes at us again.

Berty freaks out. 'GET THAT THING AWAY FROM ME!' he screams.

The glowing bee is zooming in for a second attack. I jump in front of Berty and shield us with my arms, but...

$^Z_Z^Z$ZIP!

Lightning fast, the zombee stabs me in the neck, squirting poison through its needle-sharp stinger. Then it's off and spiralling around us, ready to attack again! I drop to the ground, clutching my neck. Priti takes over, and, as the big bug flies towards us, she swings her satchel, sending the zombee spinning on to the road.

Berty Crump's eyes are the size of saucers. He is frozen with fear.

I feel sick.

'Mel! You've turned yellow!' Priti cries.

But there are worse things to worry about because the zombee is shaken but not dead. Normal bees can only sting once, and then they die. Their stingers remain in whatever they've stung, so their guts are pulled out when they fly away. But I've got a horrible feeling these zombees are like queen bees and wasps — they can sting over and over again. The zombee waggles its antennae and buzzes furiously, preparing to launch for a final attack!

GRARRZZZZZ!

'SAVE ME, PLEASE, I DON'T WANT
TO DIE!' Berty sobs. Like an angry
helicopter, Priti prepares to defend us again
with her satchel whirling above her head.

The zombee is zizzing its
wings, but it doesn't get
time to take off before...

...a lorry splatters it.

Priti and Berty stare at the splattered zombee while I lie curled up on the pavement. My head is spinning, and I feel sick.

'What sort of weird bee was that?' Berty splutters.

I'm in no mood for questions, and, anyway, I'll give away my secret if I tell them what I know. I must keep quiet.

'Forget the bee!' Priti snaps. 'We need to help Mel!'

Meanwhile, in a secret laboratory on the edge of town...

IDIOTS! YOU SORTED THE SICKNESS, BUT YOU'VE CREATED ANOTHER DISASTER! THIS YELLOW DRIBBLING DISORDER IS IN THE NEWPAPERS!

It was most unfortunate, sir, but we've tweaked the mix and our Formula Bee spray is now totally problem-free!

NO SICKNESS?

No, sir!

NO DRIBBLING?

No way!

NO
YELLOW
FACES?

Definitely not! We're spraying the plants now, and Batch Three will be 100% safe!

WELL, OK, IF YOU ARE ABSOLUTELY SURE THAT THERE WILL BE NO MORE ILLNESS ISSUES. I CAN'T AFFORD TO WAIT ANY LONGER – IT'S TIME TO SELL TO THE SUPERMARKETS!

⬡⬡⬡⬡⬡⬡⬡

A woman answers the door.

'Berty! There you are. The school rang to say...'

The woman stares at me. I'm not sure if my face is still yellow but I'm clutching my neck. 'Is your friend OK?' she asks.

Berty's swagger has disappeared.

'You won't believe this, Janet, but we were attacked by a giant bee, and Mel got stung and turned yellow, and Priti whacked it and a lorry squished it, and ...and can they come in, please?'

Janet looks worried. 'Sir Crispin doesn't...'
But then she changes her mind. 'Look, I
don't know what this is about, but Mel's
neck looks sore. Come in and let's take a look.'

Crump Mansion is massive. The kitchen is
bigger than the whole of our flat! Janet
dabs antiseptic cream on the sting, then
covers it with a plaster.

'Thanks, Mrs Crump,' I say.

'I'm not Mrs Crump!' Janet laughs. 'I
cook and clean and look after Berty.'

'Oh, sorry!' I might feel a bit embarrassed,
but at least I don't feel ill any more.
The sickness has passed.

Janet smiles. 'Sir Crispin won't be back
until late. Why don't you show your friends
around, Berty? Sort your hoodie out, leave
their bags here, and I'll organize some tea.'

'Er, OK,' Berty says, fiddling to turn his hoodie round the right way. He looks embarrassed. Perhaps he's remembering his stuck-up-superstar-celebrity act at school. I think he knows we weren't impressed. 'Are you cool with that?' he asks, sheepishly?

We leave our bags in the kitchen and follow Berty. He leads us through a big hall and into a living room crammed with paintings, antique clocks, china ornaments, and a huge fireplace. We go back in the grand hall and climb a spiral staircase.

Berty's bedroom has the biggest computer screen we've ever seen. Three guitars hang on the wall, next to shelves of comic books and computer games. His bed is king-size, and there are bowls of toffees and jelly beans scattered around the room.

'Help yourself,' Berty says. 'I'm sick of eating sweets.'

The computer bleeps, and the huge screen lights up. Berty gasps. He looks at Priti and me, then back at the screen.

'It's...it's Uncle,' he splutters.

But why is he flustered?

'I...I need to get this...'

Priti and I exchange glances. Berty clicks the accept button, and Sir Crispin Crump's face fills the screen. And what a face! Under his large nose sprouts a bushy moustache, and sitting on his head is the most ridiculous wig in the world!

'Er, hi, Uncle,' Berty says.

'Trouble at school? Are you ill? What did you eat for lunch?' Crispin Crump barks. 'Turn your camera on, boy. I want to see you!'

Unhappy Berty clicks the button, and his face appears in a smaller screen. Sir Crispin immediately seems more cheerful. 'Ha! You don't look ill. That's a relief! I was worried that... Yes, well, never mind. HANG ON A MINUTE...'

He's switched back to being angry.

'WHO'S THAT BEHIND YOU? I CAN
SEE THEM ON THE SCREEN! EH?'

'It's...just...some friends, Uncle...'
Berty whimpers.

'WHAAAT? You've brought horrible
children into my house? How dare you?
I hope they haven't stolen anything
...You haven't been snooping in my office,
have you?' he growls.

'No, Uncle...they aren't...We were just...' Berty stammers.

'I buy you all these superstar clothes, and guitars and bowls of sweets, and this is how you repay me?' Crump barks. 'I want them out of my house, and you can forget about that silly *Tons of Talent* show. The producer told me YOU'RE RUBBISH!'

There's a click, and Sir Crispin Crump's angry face disappears.

Priti and I look across at Berty, who has slumped down on the edge of the bed. His shoulders droop as he stares at the carpet.

'So now you know,' he says, looking up with sad eyes. 'My uncle is not a nice man. He buys me stuff to keep me quiet, but he doesn't spend any time with me. He's busy and bossy and... I don't actually like him very much.'

'Why are you here?' Priti asks.

'It's my mum,' Berty says. 'She had an operation and was in hospital for ages. She couldn't look after me, so I came here. I thought it would be cool — as long as I don't bother Uncle Crispin, he says I can have what I want, but... well, you get sick of that after a while. Mum's back home now but not well enough to look after me yet. I SO want to go home.'

'You seem happy at school,' I say. 'The kids think you're great!'

Berty Crump gives half a smile. 'Yeah, well...'

 'Norman Crudwell worships you!' Priti laughs to cheer up Berty.

'Crudwell's an idiot,' Berty says. 'But you two... Thanks for saving me from that monster bee. That was pretty cool.'

The computer screen lights up again, and Berty clicks the button. It's only Janet.

'Cake and cola!' she says, inviting us back down to the kitchen.

'Perhaps we'd better go,' I say, but Berty shakes his head.

'You might as well stay,' he says. 'Janet makes pretty good cakes.'

We're sitting on bar stools, munching big slabs of cherry cake, while Janet opens the fridge for cans of cola.

90

And there they are. Not the cola cans but hexagonal jars — a whole shelf of them, and this time we can read the labels.

'What's in those jars?' I ask casually.

'Some sort of honey,' Berty says. 'They're something to do with Uncle's new business, but we mustn't touch them.'

Hmmm, I wonder why? I think.

Priti's seen them too. We'll discuss it later.

'Where is your uncle's business?' she asks.

'Frogmarsh Lane, I think,' Berty says.

A shiver runs down my zombee-stung neck. The field of giant flowers and the dark factory!

It's the only building in the lane, so the factory must be Crispin Crump's new business. Time to go home and think this through, I reckon.

'I think we'd better go,' I say. 'We don't want you to get into any more trouble.'

'Nah, I'll be OK,' Berty says. He let his mask of confidence slip for a few minutes, but he seems to have put it back on.

Halfway down the path, we turn to look back.

'Hope your mum gets better soon!' Priti calls.

But Berty Crump has already disappeared indoors.

⬡⬡⬡⬡⬡

We're down the road and out of sight.

'That was unexpected!' Priti says. 'He seems almost normal at home!'

'Yeah,' I say. 'I guess things aren't always as they seem.'

'And what about that massive bee?' Priti asks. 'It's like the one on the TV news!

93

Where do they come from?'

'No idea,' I lie. It's time to change the subject. 'Did you spot the jars?'

'Of course I did! Is Crump making the horrible honey? Should we tell somebody?'

'Not yet,' I say. 'There's something important I need to do first.'

I wish I could tell Priti everything, but I mustn't give away my secret.

So I'm in my bedroom, writing a list and getting my thoughts in order:

Notes on Zombees and Horrible Honey

1. The illness at school only happens when Mrs Sweed serves honey puddings.

2. The hexagonal jars that she threw in the bin were identical to the honey jars in Sir Crispin's fridge, and we heard Mrs Sweed arguing with her son about testing out the honey.

3. Berty said the honey is to do with his Uncle's new company. Is he using schoolchildren as guinea pigs to test it?

4. The dark factory must *be* Sir Crispin Crump's because there is only one big building in <u>Frogmarsh Lane.</u>

5. So there MUST *be* a connection between the horrible honey and the zombees!

6. I WILL INVESTIGATE!

I'm still trying to puzzle it out at tea when Mum interrupts my thoughts.

'How are your bees, love?' she asks. 'Sorry I haven't been around much to help.'

'They're doing OK,' I say. 'Making lots of honey!'

'I'm so proud of you,' Mum says. 'You've stuck with your bees despite our trouble-making neighbours, and you're doing so well with your new swarm. Everything seems to have worked out, doesn't it?'

'Totally!' I say, but that's not what I'm thinking. There's work to be done.

97

It's like whoever or whatever is turning
me into a bee can read my thoughts,
because the smoker has worked its magic
again. It's just me and 998. We're on a
spying mission, buzzing across town to the
dark factory.

'We must hide as soon as we get inside,'
I say. 'The zombees will smell that we're
not one of them, and we don't want
another fight.'

But there's a problem when we arrive.
The factory doors and windows are shut
tight. Getting inside is going to be tricky.
The only entrance is a round window,
high up, where the glowing zombees come
and go. We hover and watch.

Lots of zombees have sizzled on the sun ball, but thousands more are busy in the factory, it seems. Some of the zombees are carrying out their dead and dropping them in the field below.

'Bees izz very clean insectz,' 998 says. 'But they'z not living long. Workz hard for a few weekz zen dies.'

99

After a while I notice there are gaps when nothing flies in or out of the building. We get closer and wait. Minutes pass...

'Now!' I say, and we zoom inside.

I can't believe my eyes – we're in a warehouse full of giant beehives.

Monster honey factory, Marzter!

BZZZ!

BZZZ!

BZZZ!

It's a city of beehives, and there are
glowing zombees everywhere! The noise is
deafening, and the smell...

'Weez should hide, Marzter,' 998 replies.

But we have spent too long admiring the view.

ZTOP! Zombees surround us.

'YOUZ SMELLZ LIKE INTRUDERZ! FOLLOW UZZ!' they shout, leading us to a beehive and pushing us inside.

I look across at 998. She looks strong and brave, and I try to be the same.

102

'MOVE!' We're pushed across the giant honeycomb floor to stand before the queen.

'I hazz heard about you bad beez!' she says. 'Youz killed my girlz! All sizzled on the zun ball!'

I try to explain. 'But they were going to...'

'GUARDZZZ!' she screams. 'KILL 'EM!'

We run as fast as our six little legs will take us. We're smaller than the zombees, but we're just as quick. Well, almost. They're close behind when we turn a corner and run into a pile of dead zombees. This is our chance.

'Lie completely still,' I tell 998. 'Pretend to be dead!'

The zombees are confused when they catch up and soon disappear to search elsewhere.

'Don't move!' I whisper, and there we lie, quietly catching our breath.

Then more zombees arrive and start dragging the dead bodies away. Are they looking for us? Do they know we're hiding in the pile? No. They think we're dead zombees! They drag us through the hive, carry us out through the round window, and drop us into the field below.

'Zombeez smell rub off on uzz, Marzter,' 998 says. 'They think weez one of them!'

Clever 998! We don't look like zombees – we're much smaller – but our 'intruder smell' has been replaced with their zombee pong! We fly up to the round window and go back inside the dark factory.

The zombees ignore us as we buzz around the warehouse. It's like we're invisible!

'Follow me!' I say. And we head off to explore the rest of the building. After flying down stairwells and along corridors, we arrive at the packing department. Towers of hexagonal jars are waiting to be filled, but the machines are silent.

There are no workers here, but we can hear muttering voices.

'Let's take a look!' I whisper, and we buzz along a corridor. The voice gets louder as we reach the end of the hall and spill out into another warehouse.

A giant room is filled with factory
workers gathered together in yellow boiler
suits, looking up at a man on a platform.

I recognize that wig!

'So what's this all about?' Sir Crispin Crump shouts down at them. 'If you've got something to say, spit it out, because this is a busy factory, and this meeting is costing me money!'

One of the workers steps out from the crowd. It's Tom Sweed.

'Thank you for allowing this meeting, Sir Crispin. We appreciate that time is money, but it's money that we want to discuss. Today is payday — the last Friday in the month — but we haven't been paid a penny for three months!'

'Yes, yes, of course I understand what you're saying,' Crump nods. 'But I've been let down by my science department! You're probably aware that we've had a few minor glitches...'

'Forgive me interrupting, sir, but they are more than "glitches" – our honey has made children sick, and you've made us swear to keep it a secret! You asked my mum to try out the honey in her school dinners. You said you wanted to make sure children liked the taste, but that wasn't true. You really wanted to see if there were any side effects... AND THERE WERE! Sickness and dribbling and yellow skin!'

No wonder Tom's mum was cross with him!

'Yes, OK, shut up, Sweed. No need to go on. Like I say, we've had to make a few small tweaks to the Formula Bee spray, and there was no need to tell anybody about it while we sorted things out, but listen – the research lab assures me that there are absolutely no more problems! Batch 3 of our special honey is going to be completely safe.'

Formula Bee spray? That must be the yellow stuff that the drones were spraying on the field. It makes flowers and bees grow huge ...It turns them into ZOMBEES! And the zombees are making masses of horrible honey...

It all makes sense.

'And because our honey will be COMPLETELY SAFE, I have some good news...
Are you ready to hear it?'

The workers mumble and shuffle their feet.

'I SAID, ARE YOU READY FOR SOME GOOD NEWS?!'
Crump screams.

'Yes, Sir Crispin!' they reply, standing to attention.

'Excellent. Well, you will be pleased to hear that I have just received an order for TEN MILLION JARS of our lovely value honey from the biggest supermarket in the country!' Crump grins.

The crowd murmurs with approval.

'Next Saturday, we will have a Grand Opening Party to promote our product. I will invite every single one of my celebrity friends, so the party will hit the headlines – IT WILL BE BIG NEWS! The world will be amazed when it hears about our terrifically cheap but wonderful honey, and that is when we will reveal the name of the company for which you have all worked so hard to make a success...'

THE BEE'S KNEES HONEY COMPANY!

The workers cheer and whoop and slap each other on the back, but Sir Crispin Crump hasn't finished.

'Of course, we won't actually allow anyone into our top-secret factory. The party will be outside, in the gardens at the front of the building. We'll gather by a big sign that'll be covered until we're ready to tell the world about the Bee's Knees Honey Company! OK? Are you with me? We're going to make LOTS of honey and LOTS of money! So this is the deal...

113

we'll close the hothouse for a week, and all you have to do is keep quiet about everything and work your socks off in the factory to get ten million jars of Batch 3 Bee's Knees Honey filled and labelled and boxed and...'

Crump leans forward over the safety rail.

...I WILL PAY YOU DOUBLE...NO - THREE TIMES WHAT YOU ARE OWED...YES, A TRIPLE BONUS!

The crowd erupts, pumping fists in the air, jumping for joy, and forming a conga chain to dance around the factory floor.

Hovering high above the happy workers, 998 and I notice Tom Sweed shaking his head and leaving the hall.

'It'z bad to tezt horrible honeyz on schoolchildrenz!' 998 says.

'Yes,' I say. 'I think he's sad and ashamed.'

'Or maybeez he knowz truth about Batch Three, Marzter!' 998 replies.

6

PLOOFFF!

I'm back on the roof.

Our mission has been a great success. I
know exactly what's going on in the dark
factory, and I know who's responsible for
the horrible honey. Crump says the honey's
safe now, but can I believe him? What
should I do? Tell the police? Maybe
Mum could help – she is the police. But
how can I explain what I know?

'Hey, Mum – sometimes I'm a bee, and
the other day I was on a spy mission
and flew in through the window of
a factory and discovered that they're
making dodgy honey. Go and arrest them!'

117

That's going to get ME locked up, not Sir Crispin Crump. Even if I could get the police to investigate, it might take weeks, and Crump needs stopping now.

I lean on the safety rail at the edge of the roof and look down. The view is great from here. There's a slight breeze, and the sky is glowing red as the sun slides down behind the distant hills. Birds are tweeting their evening songs in the parks and gardens that stretch away to the edge of town. I relax and think.

I can't do this on my own, but perhaps, with help from my friends and my bees, we can stop Sir Crispin Crump together. An idea starts to form in my head. In ten minutes it has become a four-part plan.

I've only got a week, so I'll need to start first thing tomorrow...

PART 1

Tom Sweed looks nervous when I ask him for help. But he's pleased that I didn't get his mum into trouble, so he agrees to 'borrow' one more jar of Bee's Knees Honey.

'It's supposed to be a secret – how come you know so much?' he asks.

'I'm friends with Berty Crump,' I say.

'Oh, right,' Tom says. 'Well, I'll get you a jar, but don't blame me if you eat it and feel ill!'

'Don't worry,' I reply. 'I'm definitely not going to eat it!'

PART 2

Berty is cross but not surprised when I tell him that it's honey from his uncle's factory that caused the illness at school.

'Doesn't surprise me,' he says. 'But it's nothing to do with me!'

'Of course not!' I say. 'But we can't let him sell dangerous honey – will you help me stop him?'

'Well… I don't know… As long as it's nothing to do with bees… I guess…'

'Thanks!' I say before Berty can change his mind, and I tell him my plan.

Berty agrees to ask his uncle if Priti can interview him at the Grand Opening Party. He'll say it's for a school project called RICH AND FAMOUS!, and Priti wants to chat with celebrities to find out how they became so… rich and famous! Helping a local schoolgirl with her project is great publicity, and I'm pretty sure Crump won't want to miss an opportunity to brag about himself!

'And one more favour…' I say.

'Er, yeah?' Berty frowns.

'Could you take a peek in your uncle's office — see if there's any…'

'Any what?' Berty scowls.

'Any evidence about his honey making people sick?'

Berty gasps. 'NO WAY! ARE YOU NUTS? HE'D KILL ME!'

That's a 'no' then.

PART 3

Priti messages Suzy Skittles.

Hi Suzy,

This is Priti Kaur from St John's. I am a friend of Berty Crump's. You gave me your business card and said to let you know if I hear anything interesting . . .

I have!

PLEASE take your TV cameras to Sir Crispin Crump's Grand Opening Party on Saturday – YOU WON'T BE DISAPPOINTED!

Best wishes,

Priti :)

PART 4

It's dark as I climb the stairs and step out on to the roof.

My match flares in the blackness as I light my smoker and start puffing.

'Let me in!' I whisper. 'We've got work to do!'

Bees don't normally fly at night, but I ask 998 for help and get it.

'Weez will stop bad beez make bad honeyz, Marzter!' she says, as our mini swarm

flies through the cold night air to the dark factory.

Each bee is carrying a little object. 'Don't drop it until I say!' I shout, as we fly over the field of flowers.

The zombees are asleep in their hives when we reach the black hothouse.

Rows of flowerpots are waiting for new seeds to be planted when the hothouse reopens. Flying low over the pots, I give the signal and we drop the little objects on to the soil, then we cluster by the big red button.

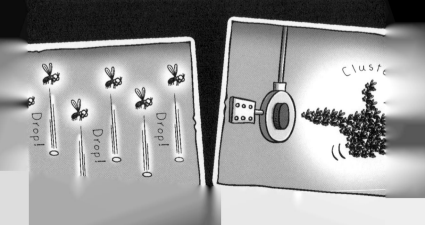

Packing tightly together, we hit the button as hard as we can, and the Formula Bee watering system hisses into action.

'Back to the hive!' I shout. 'But keep away from the yellow spray!'

We glide through the open gates of the freshly-painted factory in Miss Springfield's electric car. Publicity-hungry Sir Crispin Crump has agreed to Priti's interview and even invited her to bring some guests on this warm Saturday afternoon.

Priti's mum and dad couldn't make it, but Miss Springfield is very pleased to be invited.

'Rich and famous people?' she asks. 'Which school project is this?'

'Er... not one of yours, Miss,' Priti splutters. 'It's just something I want to write about.'

Miss Springfield smiles. 'Wonderful! A schoolchild who sets her own homework. Very unusual!'

We park and join the other guests, who are gathering next to a huge sign covered in a sheet of shiny, yellow silk.

Berty Crump appears.

'Hello, Berty!' Miss Springfield says. 'What a terrific event – your uncle is such a clever chap!'

But Berty just stares at the ground, with his hands in his pockets. He's not happy. Has he changed his mind? Has he snitched on us and told his uncle about our plan?

'Look at all the celebs!' Priti gasps, as we wander around spotting footballers, actors, and musicians from the television.

A brass band is playing jolly music, but they are struggling to be heard above the laughter and chatter of the growing crowd.

I'm watching the car park filling up fast with expensive motors when I notice a police car. It's Mum!

'No harm in checking that everybody's safe and well!' she says, walking over to shake hands with Miss Springfield. 'Just fancied having a nose, actually!' she winks, and we all laugh.

Suddenly there's a roar from above, and we gasp as an old-fashioned biplane swoops past trailing a long banner.

CRISPIN'S GRAND OPENING PARTY!

But the gasps are soon replaced with more laughter and chatter. As the plane disappears, there are high-pitched squeaks and whistles while a worried-looking man tests the sound system. Then Sir Crispin Crump is handed a microphone, and he steps on to the stage.

'Welcome, one and all, to my grand opening! I'm delighted that you are able to share our little celebration today. In a minute, the mystery will be over, and I will reveal the name of my new company, but first, I have a surprise for you!'

Crispin Crump raises his hands to calm the excited crowd.

'Believe me — I'm keen to encourage youngsters with their schoolwork, so I have agreed to do a little interview with Priti Kaur from St John's. Priti is interviewing successful celebrities and businessmen for a school project called ... RICH AND FAMOUS!...and as you all know, I am both of these things! Please give Priti a huge round of applause — she's a great girl!'

We clap loudly as Priti steps up on to the stage. She has her satchel over her shoulder and is clutching her list of questions.

I look across — Berty Crump is staring up at the stage with a look of terror.

Crump smiles smugly and hands Priti a microphone. 'So, young lady, you want to know how I became rich and famous? Well, ask away!'

'Th-th-thank you, Sir Crispin. M-m-my first question is...'

I bite my lip and clench my fists. Is Priti brave enough? Will she follow our plan? Mum, Miss Springfield, and two hundred famous faces are staring up at the stage with big smiles.

Sir Crispin Crump is pleased to see that Priti is holding the list of questions he supplied. But he's NOT pleased when she folds the list and puts it in her satchel.

'Is it true, Sir Crispin,' Priti says, looking confident now, 'that your new factory is producing honey that gives people yellow faces?'

There are murmurs and chuckles from the audience. What sort of question is this? Crump's mouth gapes open like a gormless goldfish.

Mum's looking puzzled. 'What is Priti talking about?' she whispers.

'Honey that makes people sick and dribble uncontrollably?' Priti asks.

HONEY THAT YOU TRICKED OUR SCHOOL COOK INTO TRYING OUT IN SCHOOL DINNERS?

The crowd gasps. Miss Springfield covers her face with her hands.

'Don't worry, Miss,' I whisper.

'WHAAAT?' Sir Crispin has found his voice. 'Honey? That was supposed to be a secret! What about the questions I gave... Where did you hear...? Yellow faces? Sickness? ABSOLUTELY NOT! We had a few teething problems — all new businesses do — but they have been sorted!'

Now it is the audience's turn to look like goldfish.

'So would you be happy, right now, to eat a sandwich made from your honey?' Priti continues.

'Of course!' Crump growls. 'IF you had one, but you don't, so how can I prove this is all nonsense?'

Priti opens her satchel and takes out a sandwich box. She pops it open and offers it to Sir Crispin.

'A freshly made honey sandwich, sir,' she says.

Crump peers down at the offering and scowls. 'Pah! Don't be ridiculous, that could be any honey!'

Priti dips into her satchel again and pulls out a hexagonal jar.

'Eh? Where did you...?' The rich and famous businessman is flummoxed, but then he spots the label. It is Batch Three – the new, supposedly safe batch of Bee's Knees Honey. 'Well, I don't see why I should play your silly games, but OK. If it proves that we're making healthy honey, of course I will eat it – with pleasure!'

Sir Crispin Crump bites angrily into the sandwich and munches furiously. It is clearly very tasty, and he is a greedy man. Growling, dribbling, and making rude slurping noises, he takes another bite. His science department has solved the health problems – how dare this girl spoil his party?

The sandwich is soon finished. With his hands on his hips, Crump burps loudly then... nothing.

I'm worried. Have we done the right thing? Will the world find out what sort of businessman Sir Crispin Crump really is?

'See, what did I tell you?' he shouts at Priti. 'Have I turned yellow? WELL, HAVE I? My factory is producing excellent honey at VERY low prices. People who can't normally afford such luxuries will be spreading it thick on their toast every morning. You should be THANKING me, young lady, not trying to make me look STUPID! Now, out of the way, as I proudly present our magnificent new sign for . . .

Suzy Skittles' TV cameras zoom in on the smiling face of Sir Crispin Crump.

But his smile is replaced with a puzzled expression that quickly changes to eyes tight shut and mouth wide open.

ACHOO!

Crump explodes with an enormous sneeze, sending a shower of yellow snot over his startled guests. Then his nose starts to run — just drips at first, but soon his nostrils are gushing yellow gunge.

We watch with horror as Crump pinches his nose to stop the flow. But he can't stop it. He's pinching hard, and a fine yellow spray showers over the audience.

I've never seen Miss Springfield so angry.

'So Priti's right! This Bee's Knees Honey really is dangerous stuff, and Sir Crispin has been POISONING OUR SCHOOL!'

Mum agrees. 'This new company should be closing, not opening, and Sir Crispin Crump MUST BE ARRESTED!'

143

She steps forward but stops when we all look up. There are screams from the crowd, and hands point at a dark cloud hovering over the factory.

'LOOK!' somebody shouts.

A SWARM OF GIANT BEES!

8

For a few seconds the crowd falls silent as the cloud swirls overhead and a buzz of angry bees fills the air. The bees swoop low over the dumbstruck guests.

Then the panic starts.

We'll be stung to death!

Let's get out of here!

Terrified partygoers run for their lives.
Some jump into cars and screech away
down Frogmarsh Lane. Others follow close
behind on foot. In a few minutes they
are gone, leaving just our little group.

Then the swarm gathers and shoots upwards,
spiralling high, and circling to join other bees
emerging from the round factory window.

Suzy Skittles is still reporting. 'After the
stunning revelation that Sir Crispin Crump
has been making cheap and dangerous
honey, his bees are now swarming and
preparing to attack!'

146

'If that swarm heads into town, we're in big trouble!' Mum says. 'How can we stop them, Sir Crispin?'

But Crump is a quivering wreck.

'I . . . I . . . had no idea they were going to swarm. They should be making honey . . . We've got ten million jars to fill . . .'

'Never mind your blasted honey!' Mum shouts. 'How can we stop those bees?'

Crump shakes his head.

'Unbelievable!' Mum says. 'You mean, you don't know what happens when hives get overcrowded?'

'Eh?... Er... well...' Crump splutters.

'THEY SWARM AND LEAVE!' Mum shouts.

Priti's talking to me. I think she says, 'Giant bees, Mel, like the one that attacked us!'

But, to be honest, I'm not really listening. I'm thinking about the flying mission I made with 998 the other night.

I SO need part four of my big plan to happen — RIGHT NOW!

'You've put the whole neighbourhood in danger!' Mum says, pulling a pair of handcuffs from her pocket. 'Sir Crispin Crump, I am arresting you...'

But before Mum can finish, Crump makes a dash for the factory.

We're hot on his heels as he disappears through the front door. Bursting in after him, we find ourselves in the entrance hall.

'He's gone!' Priti gasps, looking around. 'And this place is massive. We'll never find him.'

Berty steps forward. He takes a sheet of paper from his back pocket and opens it out. 'You might need this,' he says. 'It's a plan of the factory, and I think there's a secret tunnel in Uncle's office.'

'So you did look for evidence after all!' I say. 'Thanks, Berty!'

Berty shrugs his shoulders. 'Yeah, well,' he mutters.

Studying the plan, it doesn't take long to find Crump's office. Inside, we see a desk, a computer, a filing cabinet, and... a little door with a carved bee in the centre.

Berty points. 'It's the door to the tunnel.'

There's a crackle from Mum's radio:

This is Bravo Oscar Bravo - officer backup will be with you in approximately twenty minutes, DI Meadly. That's two-zero minutes - there's a traffic jam blocking our way!

'Twenty minutes? I need them here now!' Mum groans, peering at the plan. 'OK, right! The tunnel leads to a field in the woods behind the factory, and I'm pretty sure that's where Crump has gone. It's too dangerous for us to follow. We'll wait for backup and direct them when they arrive.'

Suzy brings her audience up to date. 'Callous Sir Crispin has escaped down a secret passage. Detective Inspector Meadly is on the scene but waiting for backup before tackling the evil entrepreneur!'

151

A cool breeze hits my face as I open the bee door and disappear into darkness.

'Melvin, come back!' Mum calls, but I can't hang around.

Melvin!

I feel my way down steep steps. At the bottom, the secret passage stretches ahead. At the far end I see light shining through a gap in the wall.

I hear footsteps behind me.

They're following me.

I run until I reach the gap in the tunnel wall and find steps leading up and out into the light. Giant flowers surround me.

A voice echoes from the tunnel entrance.

'COME BACK!'

I run. Pushing my way through the jungle of flowers, I emerge in a clearing. Straight ahead is the black hothouse, and it is bulging and shaking.

In the centre, the control tower rises up, with a swirling mass of zombees buzzing around the sun ball. The smashed bulb has been replaced, but something violent is happening in the rattling hothouse below. There's a loud crackle, then the power cuts and the sun ball fades to grey.

The bees peel away and dive to attack.

Swatting them away, I crouch and gather a handful of stones, but then stop and look up. A whirring noise, different from the buzz of the bees, has caught my attention.

It's Crump. He's removed a spray tank from one of the drones and climbed on board. Twiddling the remote control, he rises off the ground.

Then somebody barges past me and jumps up to catch one of Crump's ankles.

'Wait, Uncle!' Berty cries. 'We have to stop your giant bees from attacking the town!'

'Get off!' Crump bellows. 'I can't fly this drone with you hanging on!'

Then the others arrive.

'Don't let go, Berty!'
we shout together. 'You're too high!'

The drone rises up above the hothouse, higher and higher until it's hovering over the sun ball.

And that's when Priti has her good idea. 'LET GO NOW, BERTY! TRUST ME – YOU'LL LAND ON THE BIG BALL!' she screams.

Berty looks down. He hesitates for a second but quickly realizes that this is his chance. He lets go and drops on to the sun ball. For now, he is safe.

But the zombees haven't finished with Crispin Crump. They're attacking him from all sides as he whizzes up and away. Then, as he disappears behind a cloud, a small black rectangular object falls from the sky and lands in a nearby hedge.

But I can't wait any longer. It's time to start what I came here for. I throw my stones at the glass hothouse.

'What are you doing?' Mum shouts.

'Don't ask. Just help me smash the hothouse!' I say, puncturing the shiny walls with my missiles.

As jagged holes appear in the glass, plant tendrils shoot out into the daylight.

'Come on!' I shout, and finally the others join in. They trust me. Still under attack from the zombees, they hurl anything they can find at the bulging building.

Finally, with a deafening clatter, the hothouse shatters and collapses.

Released from their glass prison, giant plants burst from the ruins and rise up. They stretch their cramped stalks and open their spiky mouths. They have sprouted from the seeds that Crudwell dropped in the playground...

Unable to resist the sweet, sticky flowers, the cloud of zombees dive for their dinner. Other zombees appear from the round factory window, lured by the tasty smell of the spiky flowers. The giant hives are emptying, and the starving Venus flytraps are ready for their dinner. The zombees are grabbed and guzzled by the carnivorous plants.

But they haven't stopped attacking. Swatting zombees away with one hand, Suzy Skittles hangs on to her microphone with the other.

While giant bees attack us from all sides, Sir Crispin Crump has escaped on a drone. Disaster seemed imminent until this forest of giant Venus flytraps started munching the big insects, in a crazed feeding frenzy. It's like something from a science-fiction horror movie — disgusting and violent and... FASCINATING!

'We should get out of here!' I shout, but we've been spectating for too long. The savage plants have guzzled every single bit of their zombee dinner, and it looks like they want us for pudding! We're grabbed by the teeth of the spiky flowers and lifted high off the ground.

ERK!

WOAH!

EEK!

GOSH!

GARGH!

OOH!

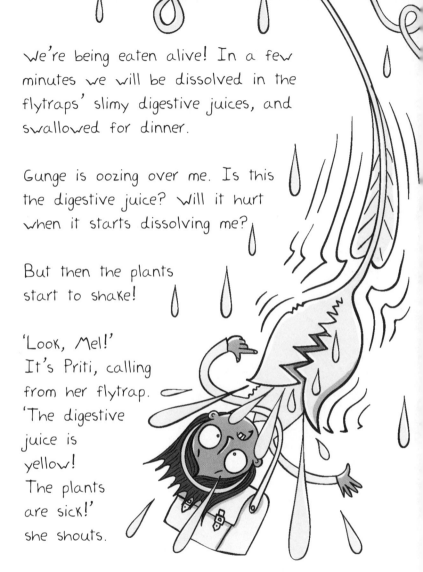

We're being eaten alive! In a few minutes we will be dissolved in the flytraps' slimy digestive juices, and swallowed for dinner.

Gunge is oozing over me. Is this the digestive juice? Will it hurt when it starts dissolving me?

But then the plants start to shake!

'Look, Mel!' It's Priti, calling from her flytrap. 'The digestive juice is yellow! The plants are sick!' she shouts.

The shaking becomes more violent. Then...

The plants are sneezing... or being sick... or dribbling, I'm not sure which.

So we're not going to be eaten after all – we're going to plummet to our deaths instead!

165

Yellow gunge is gushing from the sick Venus flytraps, with big pools collecting on the ground. So we land with a *sploop*, not a crunch.

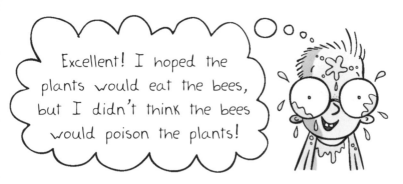

Excellent! I hoped the plants would eat the bees, but I didn't think the bees would poison the plants!

Looking around, I notice that we're all yellow! Partly from gunge, but also from the painful stings we suffered in the zombee attack.

'Is everybody OK?' Mum asks. 'Mel, are you hurt?'

'A few stings, but I'm all right...' I say.

HELP!

We look up. It's Berty.

I'M SLIPPING!

The sun ball has been splattered with gunge, and Berty is struggling to grip the curved surface. He's almost as high as Meadow Tower. If he falls, he will die.

'Keep still, Berty!' Miss Springfield calls. 'I'll save you!'

She has found the black object that landed in the hedge. It's the remote control for the drone, and Miss Springfield knows how to fly it!

'It's still in range!' she says.

Looking up, we
watch a speck in
the sky grow bigger as
Miss Springfield flies the
drone towards us.

Sir Crispin Crump! Without the remote,
he'd been whizzing about in the clouds
until Miss Springfield took over the controls.

Even from a distance, Sir Crispin Crump
looks defeated. Like us, he is yellow, and
stung and battered by the zombees.

Miss Springfield skilfully hovers the drone
over the sun ball.

169

'Grab your nephew and hold him tight, Sir Crispin!' Mum commands, in her best police voice. 'Miss Springfield will bring you back to earth!'

A few minutes later, we're all smiling. We feel sick and dizzy from the stings, but we're safe, and that's all that matters.

The hugging begins.

Mum squeezes me tight. 'You disobedient ...BRAVE BOY!' she says.

Miss Springfield wraps her arms around Priti and Berty.

But Berty shrugs her off. 'I'm OK, Miss,'
he says, and glares at his uncle.

We could have been killed! You're a monster –
a GREEDY monster, and you don't care about
anything except yourself and your money!

Sir Crispin Crump just growls.

Miss Springfield tries to lighten things
up. 'It certainly was a frightening
experience, Berty! But the danger's over –
everybody's safe, and we just need...'

'A bath?' Mum suggests, and we all
laugh. Then her radio crackles into life.

This is Bravo Oscar Bravo - traffic has cleared, and we'll be with you in two minutes, DI Meadly, over!

Thank you, Bravo Oscar Bravo - situation under control, felon apprehended, but lots of towels required, over and out!

I'm not sure how, but my plans seems to have worked rather well. I'd hoped, when the flytraps had grown big enough, they might burst out of the hothouse on their own and eat the zombees, but it turns out they needed a bit of help, from our stone throwing.

Priti sploshes over to me. She looks suspicious. 'Did you know there were giant Venus flytraps in that greenhouse?'

'Er...how could I possibly have known that?' I say.

'Yeah, well...' Priti replies, and a smile breaks through the yellow gunge on her face.

I don't think she totally believes me.

Epilogue

Sir Crispin Crump is lucky. He wasn't sent to prison, but he does have a new job. Dropping crumpled cans and empty crisp packets into his bag, he

shuffles along in shame. Crump has been sentenced to a year of litter-picking in the town centre, and the Bee's Knees Honey Company has closed.

Berty Crump is happy. He has faced his fear of bees, stood up to his awful uncle, and is now back home with his mum. He has decided not to be a celebrity after all.

Miss Springfield is very pleased. She was allowed to keep the big spray drone. It's much bigger than the little one she flies in her garden.

Priti Kaur is confused. So Crump had developed a spray that grew giant flowers and giant bees and, of course, big bees make big amounts of honey. She gets that bit — and also that chemicals in the spray were poisoning the nectar and pollen in the giant flowers, making the honey dangerous to eat; the school puddings proved that.

But where did Mel's plan to chuck stones at the hothouse come from? How did he know what was in there? Is he hiding something?

And I'm hungry. 'These cakes are yummy!'
I say, and I pour some more juice.

'So tell me all about it,' Daisy says. 'I
watched Suzy Skittles' TV report. You and
your friends are heroes!'

'Yeah, well,' I say, not wanting to explain
too much. 'It was those big Venus flytraps
that saved everybody...and Miss Springfield,
of course.'

'Yes, she was SO skilful flying the drone,
and your friend Priti deserves a medal!'
Daisy says. 'I don't know where she got

her information, but she certainly stopped Crump with his evil plant spray and horrible honey!'

I nod. Priti's interview was amazing, and I'm happy for her to get the glory, but our story doesn't have a completely happy ending. The Bee's Knees Honey Company might not be making any more Formula Bee spray, but there have been new reports of local beehives dying.

'It's not over, is it?' I ask.

Daisy shakes her head. 'I'm afraid not, Mel. Lots of hives on the edge of town have died, and Dan says the same is happening all around the world.'

I think about my precious bees.

'Is it just the chemicals that farmers are using?' I ask.

'Maybe,' Daisy sighs. 'Scientists are trying to find out. But whatever it is, they think it's going to get worse!'

'What do you mean?' I ask.

Daisy walks over to the window and looks down the garden to her hives. She shakes her head sadly. Then she turns.

'We're heading for disaster, Mel,' she whispers.

Top Tips for Helping Bees:

1. Grow plants for bees such as:

lavender   poppies   sunflowers   foxgloves

2. Don't pull up all your weeds. Bees love to feed on:

clover   dandelions   thistles

3. Try to buy honey from a local bee-keeper. You'll be helping the bees in your neighbourhood, and it's likely to be pure honey that doesn't contain other ingredients like some honey in supermarkets does.

LOCAL HONEY

4. Don't use pesticides and weedkillers in your garden. Chemicals can harm bees, and birds will go hungry if the insects they need to feed on have been poisoned.

5. Honeybees and bumblebees live in colonies, but there are other bees that live a solitary life. Here are some simple instructions to make a bee house. Solitary bees, will lay their eggs in the tubes. The eggs will grow into new solitary bees, which will pollinate flowers and help keep Planet Earth healthy!

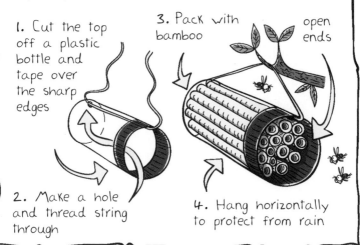

1. Cut the top off a plastic bottle and tape over the sharp edges

2. Make a hole and thread string through

3. Pack with bamboo

open ends

4. Hang horizontally to protect from rain

About the Author

Tony De Saulles worked as a book designer before turning to illustration and writing. He lives in the countryside and is learning to be a bee-keeper.

Tony has been illustrating Scholastic's best-selling Horrible Science series for 20 years and sold more than ten million copies in over thirty countries.

Bee Boy is his first project with Oxford University Press.

www.tonydesaulles.co.uk

Acknowledgements

Thanks to Liz, Gill, Lizzie, Hannah, Hattie and Fraser at OUP for their enthusiasm, help and guidance. Love and special thanks to my wife Janet for honest feedback on first drafts and for backing my arty ambitions for the past three decades.

Look out for book 3!

Curse of the Vampire Mites

Here are some other books that we think you'll love!